IT'S MY STATE!

OHIO

Joyce Hart

Lisa M. Herrington

Marshall Cavendish Benchmark

New York

Published by Marshall Cavendish Benchmark
An imprint of Marshall Cavendish Corporation

Website: www.marshallcavendish.us

Other Marshall Cavendish Offices:
Marshall Cavendish International (Asia) Private Limited, 1 New Industrial Road, Singapore 536196 • Marshall Cavendish International (Thailand) Co Ltd. 253 Asoke, 12th Flr, Sukhumvit 21 Road, Klongtoey Nua, Wattana, Bangkok 10110, Thailand • Marshall Cavendish (Malaysia) Sdn Bhd, Times Subang, Lot 46, Subang Hi-Tech Industrial Park, Batu Tiga, 40000 Shah Alam, Selangor Darul Ehsan, Malaysia

Library of Congress Cataloging-in-Publication Data
Hart, Joyce, 1954-
Ohio / Joyce Hart and Lisa M. Herrington.—2nd ed.
p. cm. — (It's my state!)
Summary: "Surveys the history, geography, government, economy, and people of Ohio"—Provided by publisher.
Includes bibliographical references and index.
ISBN 978-1-60870-524-5 (print) — ISBN 978-1-60870-702-7 (ebook)
1. Ohio—Juvenile literature. I. Herrington, Lisa M. II. Title.
F491.3.H37 2012
977.1—dc22 2010044334

Second Edition developed for Marshall Cavendish Benchmark by RJF Publishing LLC (www.RJFpublishing.com)
Series Designer, Second Edition: Tammy West/Westgraphix LLC
Editor, Second Edition: Emily Dolbear

All maps, illustrations, and graphics © Marshall Cavendish Corporation. Maps and artwork on pages 6, 26, 27, 75, 76, and back cover by Christopher Santoro. Map and graphics on pages 8 and 42 by Westgraphix LLC.

The photographs in this book are used by permission and through the courtesy of:
Front cover: Andre Jenny/Alamy and Dennis MacDonald/Alamy (inset).
Alamy: Mike Briner, 4 (left); William Leaman, 4 (right); Peter Arnold, Inc., 5; Todd Bannor, 9; Tom Till, 10; Daniel Dempster Photography, 11 (top); Danita Delimont, 11 (bottom); Terry Vacha, 12, 71; Marvin Dembinsky Photo Associates, 13; BARNpix.com, 15 (top); redbrickstock.com, 15 (bottom); First Light, 17; John E Marriott, 18 (left); Cuileandale, 19; Jeff Greenberg, 20, 43, 50, 74; The Art Archive, 24; North Wind Picture Archives, 25, 28, 30, 33, 35, 65; Kevin Parsons, 34; Stan Rohrer, 42, 52; dmac, 45; Jeremy Sutton-Hibbert, 48; David R. Frazier Photolibrary, Inc., 51; Oz Digital, 54; SG cityscapes, 56; Trevor Walker, 58; American Farm Life, 60; Jim Snyders, 63; Carol and Mike Werner, 64; View Stock, 68 (left); Linda Sikes, 68 (right); Ken Lucas/Visuals Unlimited, 69. ***Associated Press:*** Associated Press, 29. ***Getty Images:*** SSPL, 36; Time & Life Pictures, 37, 47 (top); Richard I'Anson, 38; AFP, 46; Film Magic, 47 (bottom), Getty Images, 53; Bloomberg, 66, 67. ***The Image Works:*** Jeff Greenberg, 40, 73; Andre Jenny, 59. ***Superstock:*** Age Fotostock, 16; Science Faction, 18 (right); Tony Linck, 22; Christie's Image, 31.

Printed in Malaysia (T).
135642

OHIO

CONTENTS

A Quick Look at OHIO

State Tree: Ohio Buckeye

Ohio is nicknamed the Buckeye State because of its many buckeye trees. The buckeye tree got its name from the Iroquois, who noticed that the nutlike seeds of the fruit looked like the eyes of a buck (a male deer). It became the state tree in 1953. The buckeye tree can grow to be 60 feet (18 meters) tall, but most of Ohio's buckeyes are about half that tall. The sports teams at Ohio State are known as the Buckeyes.

State Bird: Cardinal

Cardinals, once rare in Ohio, live throughout the state today. The cardinal was adopted as the state bird in 1933. The feathers of the male are usually red, while the female's feathers tend to be brown. A cardinal also has a distinctive tuft of feathers on the top of its head.

State Mammal: White-tailed Deer

Although white-tailed deer are common throughout Ohio, most roam in the southeastern woodlands. They are the state's largest game animals. In 1988, the white-tailed deer was designated the state mammal.

★ **Nickname:** The Buckeye State ★ **Statehood:** 1803
★ **Population:** 11,536,504 (2010 Census)

State Insect: Ladybug

In 1975, the ladybug, officially known as the ladybird beetle, was named Ohio's state insect. At the time, legislators compared the ladybug's qualities to the people of Ohio. They called the ladybug "proud and friendly" and "extremely industrious." Gardeners appreciate ladybugs because they feed on insects that can harm crops.

State Reptile: Black Racer

The black racer snake, named the state reptile in 1995, can be found throughout Ohio. Because the black racer eats disease-carrying rodents that damage crops, it is known as the "farmer's friend." Some of these speedy hunters have been recorded going 10 miles (16 kilometers) per hour.

State Fruit: Tomato

Tomatoes are an important crop in Ohio, a leading producer of tomato products. Elementary school students worked to help pass the bill that made the tomato Ohio's official state fruit in 2009.

OHIO
LAKE ERIE
ROCK AND ROLL HALL OF FAME
Toledo
Bowling Green
SANDUSKY BAY
Sandusky
Cleveland
CUYAHOGA RIVER
Warren
MAUMEE RIVER
Findlay
SANDUSKY RIVER
MILK
Youngstown
Akron
INDIAN TRAIL CAVERNS
Mansfield
Lima
Canton
Marion
GRAND LAKE ST. MARYS
CAMPBELL HILL
Steubenville
Newark
Columbus
Greenville
MUSKINGUM RIVER
GREAT CIRCLE EARTHWORKS
Springfield
Dayton
SCIOTO RIVER
Marietta
GREAT MIAMI RIVER
WAYNE NATIONAL FOREST
SALT
Cincinnati
OHIO RIVER
LEO PETROGLYPH STATE MEMORIAL
SERPENT MOUND STATE MEMORIAL
Portsmouth
WAYNE NATIONAL FOREST
OHIO RIVER
N
W
E
S

The Buckeye State

Located in the Midwest, Ohio is known as the Buckeye State. It gets its nickname from the many buckeye trees native to the region.

Ohio is a medium-size state. With a land area of 40,948 square miles (106,056 square kilometers), Ohio ranks thirty-fifth among the states. Ohio is divided into eighty-eight counties.

From rolling hills to flat plains and sandy beachfronts, Ohio is a combination of landscapes. The eastern border of the state starts as rolling plateaus (raised land) and slowly settles into flat plains toward the west. The state's northern border is largely made up of a long beachfront along Lake Erie. The majestic Ohio River cuts a curving trail from east to west across Ohio's southern border.

Quick Facts

OHIO BORDERS

North	Lake Erie Michigan
South	Kentucky West Virginia
East	Pennsylvania West Virginia
West	Indiana

How Ohio Was Formed

Massive sheets of ice called glaciers moved slowly across much of Ohio about 15,000 years ago, during the last Ice Age. The glacial movement changed the landscape in many ways, flattening hills, filling valleys, and carving out the state's four primary land regions. Those regions are the Appalachian Plateau, the Bluegrass Region, the Till Plains, and the Lake

Ohio Counties

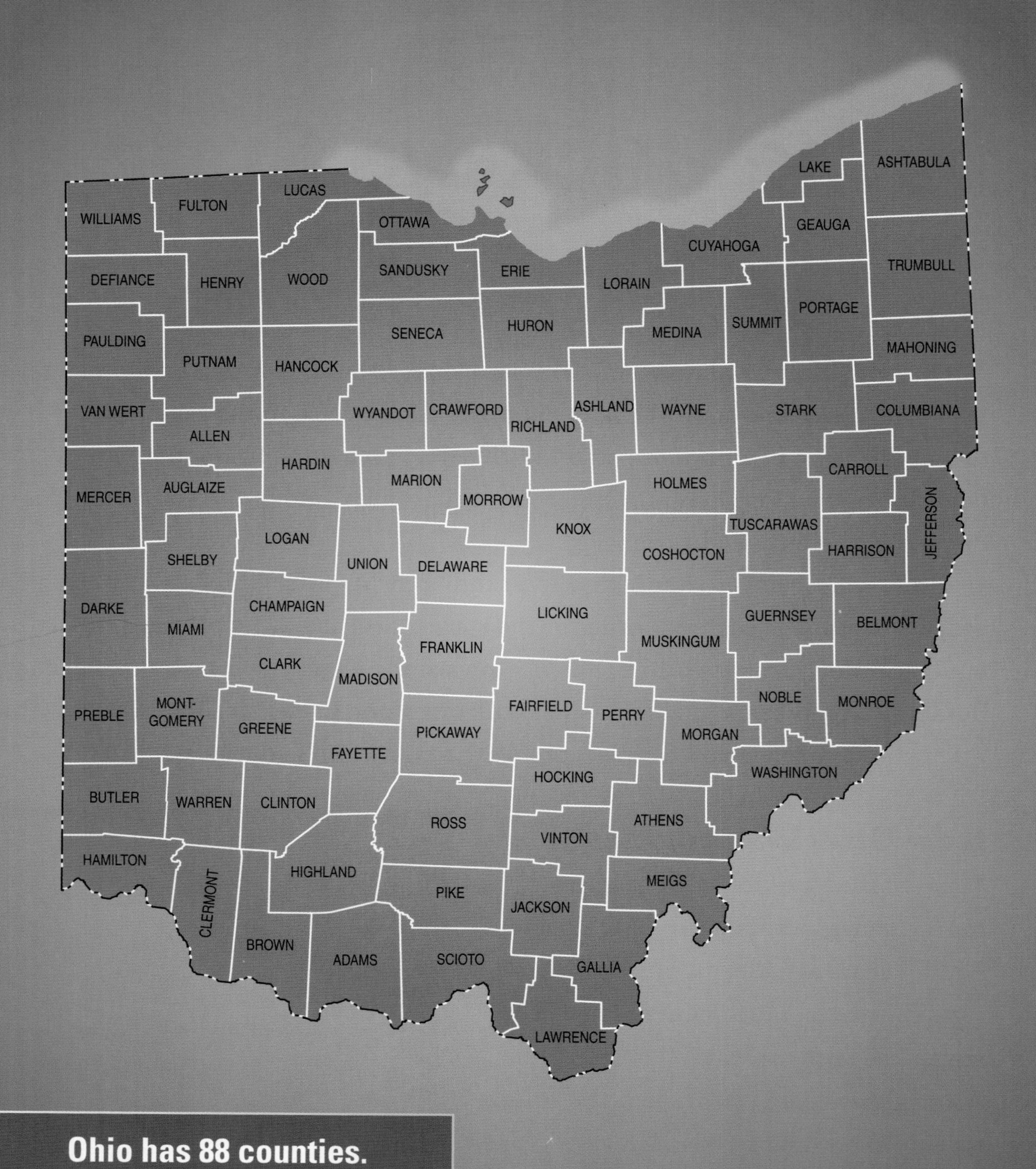

Ohio has 88 counties.

A riverboat ship cruises along the Ohio River, which forms the state's southern border.

Plains. As the glaciers melted, Lake Erie formed and then overflowed. The excess water eventually created a small stream, which grew in size over time and is today the Ohio River.

The Appalachian Plateau

Most of the eastern half of Ohio is made up of the Appalachian Plateau. The northern part of this area contains rolling hills and valleys. The southern part of this area contains some of the steepest hills and deepest valleys in what is considered the most rugged part of the state. It is not a farming area because the soil is not very fertile. Although forests once covered most of the state, many of them have been cut down. But some of the largest remaining forests, such as Wayne National Forest, still exist on the Appalachian Plateau.

Much of Ohio's richest mineral deposits are located on the Appalachian Plateau. Coal, for instance, was first found in Jefferson County, on Ohio's eastern border. Since that discovery, Ohio has become one of the country's biggest coal producing states. Natural gas and oil are also found there.

Quick Facts

GREAT RIVER

The name *Ohio* comes from the Iroquois word *O-hy-o*, meaning "great river." The Iroquois first used the word to describe the river, and it later became the state's name.

Vibrant sumac grows in Wayne National Forest, located on the Appalachian Plateau.

The city of Marietta is on the southern part of the Appalachian Plateau. East Liverpool, famous for its pottery, is also situated on the Appalachian Plateau. Athens, Hocking, and Perry are some of the area's main coal-producing counties. Akron sits at the northern edge of the plateau. Its population is about 207,000, making it Ohio's fifth-largest city.

The Bluegrass Region

When someone hears the term "Bluegrass Region," Kentucky usually comes to mind. But this region spills north from Kentucky into Ohio, too. Also referred to as the Lexington Plain, the Bluegrass Region, located in the southern part of the state, is the smallest land area in Ohio. It contains rolling hills that are covered in a thin layer of fertile soil. Adams Lake, a beautiful recreation area, and the Shawnee State Forest, one of the state's largest forests, are found here.

The Till Plains

The Till Plains, south of the Lake Plains, make up most of western Ohio. Although the region typically has low, rolling hills, both the highest and the lowest points in Ohio are located here. Campbell Hill, in Logan County, rises 1,550 feet (472 m) into the sky. It is the state's highest point. At the

The Till Plains in western Ohio is one of the most fertile farming areas in the United States.

southwestern corner of the state, along the Ohio River near Cincinnati, is Ohio's lowest point, measuring only 455 feet (139 m) above sea level. The hills of these plains are made up of soil and rocks that retreating glaciers left there as they melted at the end of the last Ice Age. Most of this area was completely covered in woodlands before white settlers moved into the region and discovered the rich soil.

The Till Plains have the most fertile soil in Ohio. The region is where most of the state's farms are located. Farmers here grow wheat, corn, and soybeans. They also raise cattle. The Corn Belt—an area where most of the corn in the United States is grown—begins in the Till Plains and extends west for many hundreds of miles.

Cincinnati, Ohio's third-largest city, was founded along the Ohio River.

The rich soil may have attracted many of the early white settlers, but in modern times, it is the large cities that draw new people. Cincinnati, Ohio's third-largest city with a population of about 333,000, lies to the south on the Till Plains. Dayton, the sixth-largest city, with about 154,000 people, is just a short drive north of Cincinnati. Columbus, the state's largest city and capital, is located in the center of the Till Plains. More than 770,000 people live in Columbus.

The Lake Plains

The Lake Plains cover the entire northern portion of Ohio. Many different kinds of fruits and vegetables grow on the region's fertile land. Most of the Lake Plains follows the shoreline of Lake Erie. In the northeastern corner of the state, the plains extend only 5 to 10 miles (8 to 16 km) south of the lake. In the northwestern corner, however, they broaden to more than 50 miles (80 km).

With a population of about 431,000, Cleveland, Ohio's second-largest city, dominates this area. Located on Lake Erie, Cleveland is a busy manufacturing and shipping center. Other cities in this region, such as Toledo, Ohio's fourth-largest city (with more than 316,000 people), and Lorain, also have ports on Lake Erie. These ports allow them to ship their products to other states and countries.

Marblehead Lighthouse is a popular landmark along Lake Erie.

The Waterways

Thousands of years ago, Ohio was covered with water. Today, much of that water has drained into tens of thousands of lakes and ponds, as well as 44,000 miles (70,800 km) of rivers and streams. All the rivers and streams in the northern quarter of the state empty into Lake Erie. The other rivers drain into the Ohio River to the south. The major rivers in the state include the Ohio, Scioto, Miami, Sandusky, Huron, and Cuyahoga.

This waterfall is located near Old Man's Cave in Hocking Hills State Park.

Lake Erie is Ohio's largest lake (although parts of the lake are in other states or in Canada). Erie is the second-smallest Great Lake, after Lake Ontario. But Lake Erie is not that small. It is the twelfth-largest freshwater lake in the world, and it extends more than 200 miles (320 km) from east to west and about 57 miles (92 km) from north to south. Thousands of years ago, Lake Erie was much deeper. Beach ridges—sandy deposits that rise above the otherwise flat ground—are noticeable in some spots along the coastal plain in northwestern Ohio. These ridges mark the ancient shoreline and show how high the lake waters used to be. Today, Lake Erie's deepest point measures only about 200 feet (60 m). Several small islands in Lake Erie—Kelleys Island and the three Bass Islands—are part of Ohio and serve as popular recreation areas.

Quick Facts

OHIO'S CAVERNS

Underground streams in Ohio helped create caverns, or caves. In 1872, two boys, Peter Rutan and Henry Homer, discovered Seneca Caverns in Bellevue. Today, the caverns are a popular attraction for visitors to the area. Ohio Caverns, in West Liberty, were discovered in 1897. They are the largest caverns in Ohio, with more than 2 miles (3.2 km) of known passageways.

THE GREAT LAKES
Lake Erie is the shallowest of the five Great Lakes. The other lakes are Superior, Michigan, Huron, and Ontario.

Ohioans enjoy other lakes, too. Some of the major lakes in Ohio are Berlin Lake, Seneca Lake, C. J. Brown Reservoir, and Grand Lake St. Marys (the largest lake entirely within Ohio).

The Climate

Ohio's climate is generally about the same for all regions of the state. This is partly due to the fact that the state has no very tall mountain ranges that can create different climate zones—either because of large differences in altitude or because the mountains block moving weather systems. When a weather system blows down from Canada or up from the Gulf of Mexico, nothing stops it from completely crossing Ohio. Sometimes, strong weather systems bring Ohioans very cold or very hot or very stormy weather. Another factor affecting the state's climate is Lake Erie, which can make northern Ohio a bit colder in the spring. In the fall, though, temperatures along the lake will be a little bit warmer than in the rest of the state.

In January, Ohioans can expect the temperature to linger around 28 degrees Fahrenheit (–2 degrees Celsius), on average, which is just a little below freezing and perfect for snow. In July, warm, humid weather, with an average temperature of 73 °F (23 °C), hangs over the state. Ohioans spend the cold winter days snuggled in warm jackets and gloves from about November until March. They have warmer and stormier days, with thunderstorms and sometimes tornadoes possible, in the spring and summer. In the fall, the days are crisp and cool.

RECORD-BREAKING TEMPERATURES
Ohio's lowest recorded temperature was minus 39 °F (–39 °C), which was measured in 1899 in Milligan, near New Lexington. The highest temperature was 113 °F (45 °C), recorded in Gallipolis in 1934.

The wettest part of the state is located in the southwest around Wilmington. Toledo and Sandusky, in the northern part of the state, receive the least amount of rain and snow. People who live in northeastern Ohio see the most snow—almost 100 inches (254 centimeters) a year.

Snow covers an old Ohio dairy and horse barn.

Wildlife

When white settlers first arrived in Ohio, forests covered much of the state. But early settlers cleared many trees to make way for farming and to build towns. Today, forests cover about one-fourth of Ohio. Forest trees include buckeyes, sycamores, maples, and oaks.

A wide range of flowers and trees grows in Ohio's forests, plains, and fields. Some of these plants produce things people can eat. The shagbark hickory tree, for example, produces nuts. This hickory tree is also the source for delicious syrup. American Indians used to make a refreshing drink from the berries of the red sumac shrub. A tree that produces a fruit called a pawpaw grows in the river valleys of Ohio. Similar to a banana, the pawpaw is long and ripens to a brown color. In 2009, the pawpaw became the state's official native fruit.

The state is also home to a variety of animals. Different types of birds, such as cardinals, chickadees, and sparrows, fly through the Ohio

Pawpaw trees—and their tasty, nutritious fruit—grow in southern Ohio.

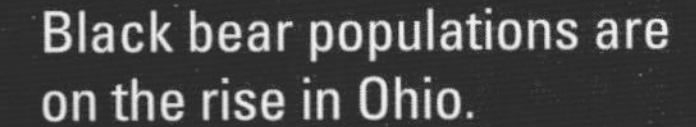

Black bear populations are on the rise in Ohio.

skies and nest in fields and trees. Cardinals, which generally do not live in thick forests, actually became much more common as forests were cleared. Fish, amphibians, and other aquatic animals live in Ohio's lakes, rivers, and streams. Ohio has snakes, turtles, salamanders, and frogs. Many of its woodland animals are small. In the forests are woodland creatures such as white-tailed deer, raccoons, opossums, squirrels, bats, and rabbits. Larger animals, such as wolves, cougars, bison, and elk, once filled Ohio's large wilderness areas, but their numbers decreased as more people moved into the area.

The black bear, for example, lived throughout the state at one time. But by the 1850s, there were no black bears left in Ohio. Black bear populations are coming back because many regions are restoring their forests. Scientists recently counted more than one hundred black bears in Ohio, and some of them were females with cubs.

Bald eagles are also making a comeback. In 1979, the state had only four nesting pairs. Today, it has more than two hundred. Bald eagles were endangered at one point, due in part to habitat loss and pesticide use. (When a type of animal is endangered, there are so few left that the animal is at risk of becoming extinct, or completely dying out.) Pesticides—chemicals that kill insects—eventually wash into the rivers and lakes and contaminate fish. Bald eagles eat the fish and are poisoned by the pesticides. Since many of the most dangerous pesticides are banned today, the health of the fish and the bald eagles is improving.

Like bald eagles, beavers were once numerous in today's Ohio. But in the 1700s and early 1800s, trappers could earn a great deal of money selling beaver skins, and huge numbers of beavers were killed. By 1830, there were few beavers left. As beaver skins decreased in popularity, Ohio's beaver population began to increase. By the 1970s, it was estimated that more than five thousand beavers lived in Ohio. Scientists today believe that the beaver population has increased to more than 25,000.

Endangered Wildlife in Ohio

Ohio has several species of plants and animals that are considered endangered. Many things threaten wildlife, including human settlement, pesticides, overhunting, and pollution.

Several bird species, including the sandhill crane, the common tern, the golden-winged warbler, and the trumpeter swan, are on the state's list of endangered animals. The trumpeter swan is white with a black beak. It is the world's largest living waterfowl. Hunted for food and feathers, trumpeter swan populations had practically disappeared by the early 1900s. By the mid–1900s, some programs to restore the trumpeter swan in the United States and Canada began. In 1996, Ohio joined a group of states that raised trumpeter swans in zoos and released several pairs into the wild. Today, the state has about seventy pairs of trumpeter swans.

The black-billed trumpeter swan is among several bird species on Ohio's list of endangered animals.

Plants & Animals

Cicada

Many Ohioans call this insect a locust, but cicadas and locusts, in fact, belong to different families of insects. The male cicada produces a mating call by vibrating its drumlike abdomen to attract females. The sound of the cicada is so much a part of Ohio summer, it would not seem like summer without it.

Weasel

Weasels live throughout the United States but their numbers are especially high in Ohio. The weasel population is so large in Ohio that the animals are hunted for their fur. Weasels live in forests and on Ohio farmlands, as long as there is water nearby. Catching and eating mice is one of the weasel's specialties.

Perch

The yellow perch, native to Ohio, can be found in lakes, ponds, and slow-moving rivers. This fish, which is golden yellow with black stripes, prefers clear water with a sandy bottom.

Persimmon Tree

Native to Ohio, the persimmon tree grows in the southern part of the state. Its delicious fruit ripens in the fall and is part of many Thanksgiving celebrations. American Indians dried persimmons and ate them throughout the winter months. Because persimmon wood is very hard, it is used by businesses that produce wood heads for golf clubs and cue sticks for billiards.

Trillium

The trillium is Ohio's state wildflower. It has three large ruffled petals and three large oval leaves. Its name comes from the Latin word for "three." Trillium flowers are found throughout Ohio in the early spring. Because a trillium blooms about the same time that robins migrate back to Ohio, the flower used to be called a "wake robin."

Scarlet Carnation

In 1876, a doctor and avid gardener named Levi L. Lamborn ran for a congressional seat against William McKinley—a fellow Ohioan who became president in 1897. Before their debates, Lamborn often gave McKinley one of his scarlet carnations. McKinley continued to wear a carnation in his lapel for luck. After McKinley was assassinated in 1901, the Ohio legislature honored him by making the scarlet carnation the state flower in 1904.

From the Beginning

Scientists and historians estimate that people have lived in what is now Ohio for about 15,000 years. The first people, called Paleo-Indians, inhabited Ohio during the last Ice Age. Paleo-Indians moved from place to place, hunting wild animals, fishing, and gathering fruits and nuts. They used flint, an important natural resource from the area, to make tools and weapons.

Over time, thick forests started to grow as warming climates melted glaciers. Continuing in the tradition of their Paleo-Indian ancestors, the Archaic people hunted and gathered food. Unlike the Paleo-Indians, however, they settled down in permanent camps. They, too, mined flint and other stones to make axes used to cut down trees, build canoes, and create decorative ornaments for spears.

Mound Builders

The Woodland Period started in today's Ohio about three thousand years ago. During this period, hunting and gathering shifted to farming. Prehistoric people started to settle into more permanent villages, create pottery, harvest crops, and build elaborate mounds with raised piles of earth and stone. The mounds, often constructed in the shape of animals and geometric figures, were used to bury the dead and other treasured items.

The first of these Woodland groups were the Adena. The Adena people were the area's first farmers. They grew crops such as squash and sunflowers. Because

Archaeologists—people who study the remains of cultures—use a screen to find artifacts at an excavation site in Chillicothe.

Quick Facts

SERPENT MOUND

Located in Adams County in southern Ohio, Serpent Mound is the largest mound in the United States. It is likely that the Fort Ancient people built it more than one thousand years ago. Resembling a huge snake, Serpent Mound is 1,330 feet (405 m) long, and visitors can see the serpent's open jaws at one end.

they needed to tend their various crops, the Adena people built small, permanent villages.

Another Woodland group of skilled mound builders, called the Hopewell, lived in the area about 1,500 years ago. They built gigantic mounds of various shapes that enclosed hundreds of acres of land. The Hopewell lived in small villages where they grew crops, fished, hunted wild game, and gathered plants. They were also superior traders. They obtained shells from the Gulf of Mexico, copper from the Great Lakes region, and a mineral called mica from the Carolinas.

From 600 CE to 1200 CE, the culture began to change. Villages grew larger, and many communities began to surround themselves with a defensive wall or ditch for protection. During this time, an important innovation—the bow and arrow—was used for hunting and as a weapon. While the Woodland people still cultivated squash and sunflowers, they began to grow corn, or maize, around 800 CE. Included among the last groups, who inhabited the land until the seventeenth century, were the Fort Ancient people in southern Ohio, the Sandusky in northwestern Ohio, and the Whittlesey in northeastern Ohio.

The Iroquois

During the 1600s, the powerful Iroquois, from the area of present-day New York, made their way into the region. The Iroquois peoples (members of a confederacy of several tribes) came in search of new hunting grounds, and they found an abundance of wildlife and edible plants in what is now Ohio. As a result, they pushed out most of the descendants of Ohio's prehistoric Indian cultures.

By the 1700s, as the Iroquois grew less powerful in what is now Ohio, other Indian groups began to move into the area. One tribe, the Huron, moved south from Canada and settled around the Sandusky River. Another American Indian group, the Miami people, came from the west. They set up villages along the rivers that now bear their name—the Great Miami and the Little Miami. Some bands of Iroquois also first moved to Ohio around this time. The Mingo were a small group of American Indians related to the Iroquois. They left the Iroquois

American Indians from the Ohio Country meet with French military leaders on the banks of the Muskingum River.

homeland in the New York area and settled mostly in eastern and central Ohio. The Lenape people, also called the Delaware, settled in eastern Ohio. The Shawnee, who were pushed out of Pennsylvania by white settlers, moved into southern Ohio.

French and English Control

European exploration of the land that is now Ohio began in the mid–1600s. For the next century, the French and the English fought over the right to claim the land referred to as the Ohio Country. This region included most of what would become Ohio as well as portions of Indiana, West Virginia, and Pennsylvania. Both the French and the English set up fur-trading companies in the region. Both wanted to control the profitable trade in the animal skins that American Indians brought to trading posts. Both tried to convince different Indian groups to join them in their wars.

Quick Facts

EUROPEAN EXPLORERS

René-Robert Cavelier, sieur de La Salle, a French explorer from Canada, was likely the first European to set foot in what is now Ohio. La Salle is believed to have explored the Ohio River as early as 1669. Based on his travels, France claimed the region. But England believed it had a right to the land, which it considered the western extent of its Atlantic coast colonies.

The final clash in this ongoing conflict between France

Fighting on the side of the British during the French and Indian War, a young George Washington marches his troops through the Ohio Country to drive out French forces.

and Great Britain was the French and Indian War (1754–1763). Britain won the war and the right to claim all of the Ohio Country (as well as almost all the rest of North America east of the Mississippi River).

PLAYING A GAME OF QUOITS

Ancient Greeks played the game of quoits (pronounced KWOITZ) more than two thousand years ago. A form of the game eventually became popular among English colonists, who brought it with them to North America. In Ohio and other states, the game of quoits developed into horseshoes.

WHAT YOU NEED

Rope or clothesline, 5 feet (1.5 m) long

Ruler

Scissors

Yarn, 12 inches (30 cm) each of two different colors

Packing or duct tape

Round wooden stake, at least 12 inches (30 cm) long (you can use a stick or a wooden dowel)

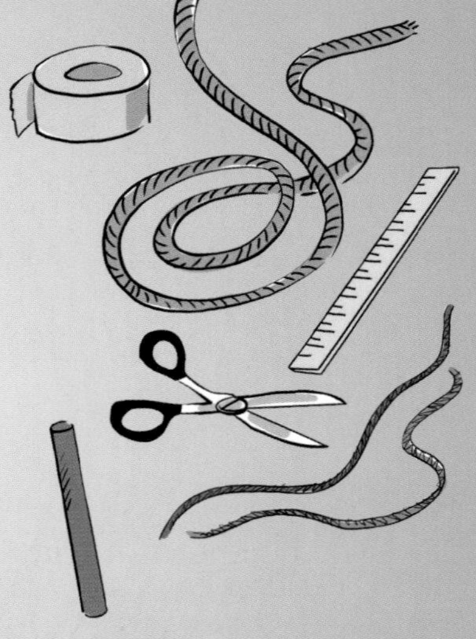

Cut the rope into four 15-inch (38-cm) pieces. Cut the yarn into four 6-inch (15-cm) pieces.

Wrap one piece of yarn around one piece of rope (see illustration on next page). Do the same with the other three pieces of yarn and rope.

Loop each piece of rope into a circle with the ends touching. Tape the ends together. Add as much tape as you need to keep the rope in a ring shape. You should have four rings of rope—two of each yarn color.

Push the stake into the ground. About 15 feet (4.6 m) away, mark a tossing line. You can use a piece of string or a branch to mark the tossing line.

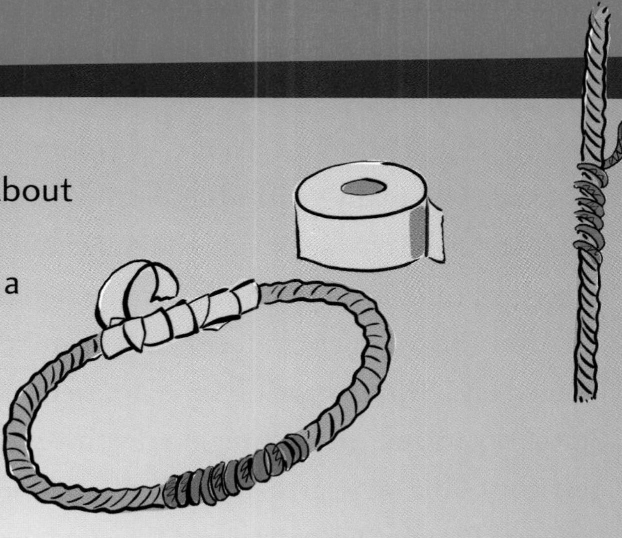

How to Play

The game is played by two people. Each player has two rope rings, or quoits, of the same color. The first player tosses his or her two quoits, one at a time, toward the stake. Then, the second player throws his or her rings.

If a quoit encircles the stake, called the hob, the player who tossed it gets 3 points. The quoit closest to (but not around) the hob scores 1 point. A player earns no points if his or her quoit lands on top of the other player's quoit.

The players take turns tossing the quoits until one of them reaches 21 points. That person is the winner!

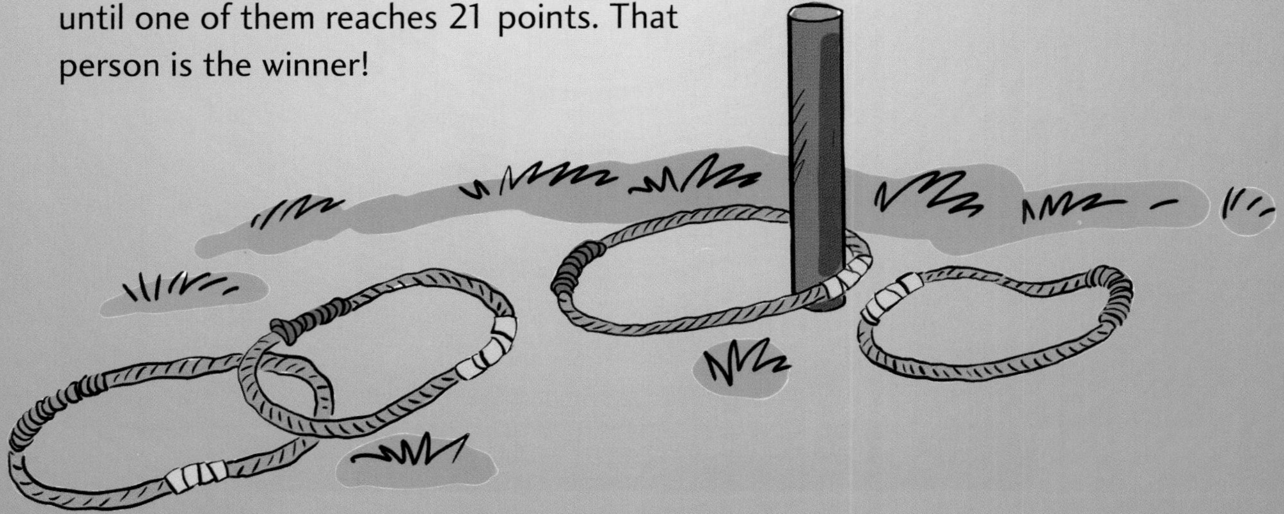

The Northwest Territory

After Britain won the French and Indian War, it tried to prevent American colonists from moving west into the Ohio Country. Britain wanted good relations with the region's Indian groups, in order to avoid costly wars and to protect its fur trade. Not many years after, however, war broke out between the American colonists and Britain. During the American Revolution (1775–1783), the American colonists fought for independence from Britain.

After the colonists won the American Revolution, the United States was formed and Britain gave up its claim to the Ohio Country. In 1787, the United States organized the vast region northwest of the Ohio River into the Northwest Territory. This large area of frontier land included the present-day states of Ohio, Indiana, Illinois, Michigan, and Wisconsin, as well as part of Minnesota.

On July 13, 1787, the Northwest Ordinance was passed. This document outlined how the Northwest Territory was to be divided and governed. The

After the American Revolution, settlers from eastern states moved into today's Ohio in search of land and a place to live.

Northwest Ordinance ultimately paved the way for Ohio to become the seventeenth state. According to the document, the U.S. Congress selected the first governor. As soon as five thousand male landowners lived in the territory, they could elect their own legislature, which included a house of representatives and a legislative council. Later, when 60,000 people lived in one portion of the territory, that portion could apply for statehood.

American settlers were eager to move into the Northwest Territory. In 1788, pioneers from New England, led by General Rufus Putnam, founded Marietta, the first permanent settlement by people of European descent north and west of the Ohio River. Marietta (named after France's Queen Marie Antoinette) was declared the first capital of the Northwest Territory. General Arthur St. Clair was appointed governor of the Northwest Territory.

Battle of Fallen Timbers

As Americans from the East settled the Northwest Territory in larger and larger numbers, the region's American Indians fought to keep their land. After several victories, in 1794, they suffered a terrible defeat at the Battle of Fallen Timbers, near present-day Toledo. The area got its name from trees that had been knocked down by a tornado. General "Mad Anthony" Wayne led an army of three thousand troops in the battle. Afterward, American Indian tribes signed the Treaty of Greenville in 1795, giving up most of their lands in Ohio.

American Indians were forced to give up most of their land in Ohio after being defeated at the Battle of Fallen Timbers.

Statehood

By 1803, the eastern portion of the Northwest Territory had enough residents for Ohio to apply for statehood. On March 1, 1803, Ohio became the seventeenth U.S. state. It was the first state carved out of the territory.

Ohio's first capital was Chillicothe. Zanesville was made the capital in 1810, but two years later, the legislature returned the capital to Chillicothe. Then, in 1816, Columbus was chosen as Ohio's permanent state capital. The capital was named after explorer Christopher Columbus.

American Indian Losses

Although Ohio was now a state, tensions between white settlers and American Indians continued. By the 1800s, many American Indian groups were suffering. More and more of their land was being taken over by white settlers and hunting for the fur trade had caused animal populations to dwindle. Many American Indians had trouble finding food.

Indian leaders were concerned about their people and the loss of their land. Shawnee chief Tecumseh and his brother, known as the Prophet, tried to unite many tribes to stop white settlers from taking their land. General William Henry Harrison, who later became president of the United States, knew of Tecumseh's plans. In 1811, Harrison's troops attacked and destroyed Prophetstown, the largest Shawnee village (located in present-day Indiana). This defeat, in what became known as the Battle of Tippecanoe, seriously weakened Tecumseh and his followers, but he did not give up.

Shawnee leader Tecumseh tried to prevent white settlers from taking land from American Indians.

In an attempt to defeat General Harrison and regain Ohio's lands, Tecumseh and his men joined forces with the British Army against the Americans when the War of 1812 (1812–1815) began. Tecumseh hoped that if the British won, they would return the land to the American Indians.

The United States fought Great Britain for control of Lake Erie during the War of 1812. In 1813, U.S. ships commanded by Lieutenant Oliver Hazard Perry won the Battle of Lake Erie, which was fought off Ohio's shores.

In Their Own Words

We have met the enemy, and they are ours.

—Oliver Hazard Perry, reporting the victory over the British at the Battle of Lake Erie to General William Henry Harrison

U.S. lieutenant Oliver Hazard Perry (holding a sword) defeated the British at the Battle of Lake Erie during the War of 1812.

Quick Facts

AMERICAN HERO

A monument to American soldier Oliver Hazard Perry (1785–1819) was erected on the Ohio Island of Put-in-Bay in Lake Erie. Hazard earned the title "Hero of Lake Erie" for leading American forces in a naval victory over the British in the Battle of Lake Erie during the War of 1812.

The victory paved the way for General Harrison to cross Lake Erie and successfully attack British and American Indian forces at the Battle of the Thames in Canada in 1813. Tecumseh was killed during the fighting. The U.S. victory essentially marked the end of the alliance among American Indian tribes that Tecumseh had worked to create.

The New State Grows

After Ohio became a state, its government encouraged settlers to move into the area. Ohio grew quickly during the nineteenth century. By 1860, more than 2 million people lived in Ohio, making it the country's third-most-populous state. Many Ohioans were farmers, who grew crops such as corn, beans, and melons and raised livestock. Farmers also planted apple and peach orchards and shipped the fruit to the East Coast. They planted tobacco, which was manufactured into smoking materials. Factories were built to process Ohio's crops. Other factories began producing farm equipment, such as tractors and reapers.

Improvements in transportation helped farming businesses, too. Paved roads made it easier to transport crops to the East Coast. The development of steamboats in the early 1800s helped to deliver products quickly to the South by way of the Mississippi River.

The building of canals also helped Ohio expand its industry and transport its goods. Workers dug the long, narrow waterways so that boats could travel over hilly terrain. In 1832, the Ohio and Erie Canal was completed, connecting Cleveland on Lake Erie and Portsmouth on the Ohio River. In 1845, the Miami and Ohio Canal opened. It connected Toledo and Cincinnati.

During the 1800s, Ohioans built canals to transport goods.

By the 1850s, railroads had become the latest improvement in transportation. They contributed to the decline of canals. Trains became a quick, cheap way to move Ohio's products throughout the country. By the 1900s, most of the canals were no longer in use.

Agriculture remained a strong industry in Ohio until the late nineteenth century. By then, other states in the West had been admitted to the Union, and Ohio farmers had trouble competing with their low prices. Many Ohioans sold their farms and moved to the thriving cities to find other types of work. Cleveland, which began as a frontier outpost, expanded into a major industrial hub. Cincinnati became the country's largest meatpacking center, earning it the nickname "Porkopolis."

Quick Facts

OHIO'S FIRST RAILROAD

Construction began on Ohio's first railroad in 1835 and was completed by 1836. It connected Toledo, Ohio, to Adrian, Michigan, and covered a distance of 33 miles (53 km). The trip took three hours.

Slavery and the Civil War

As Ohioans were getting used to life in their new state, the country faced a serious conflict between Northern states and Southern states over the issue of slavery. As a "free state," Ohio did not allow slavery. By the early 1800s, most Northern states no longer allowed or were in the process of ending the practice of slavery. Millions of people, descendants of Africans captured and forcibly brought to the Americas, were slaves in the Southern states. A very strong antislavery movement developed in Ohio in the decades before the Civil War (1861–1865). Ohio resident Harriet Beecher Stowe wrote the famous antislavery book *Uncle Tom's Cabin*, which was published in 1852.

Many enslaved people in the South tried to escape to freedom by heading to Canada. They often traveled through Ohio, where there were many abolitionists, or people who opposed slavery. Ohioans helped slaves escape along the Underground Railroad. This was not an actual railroad but a secret network of people and hiding places that helped runaway slaves travel to freedom. People who disagreed with slavery hid runaway slaves in their homes. They fed, clothed, and cared for them before sending them on the next leg of their journey.

Quick Facts

THE RANKIN HOUSE

The Rankin House in Ripley, Ohio, was a famous hiding place on the Underground Railroad. From 1825 to 1865, Presbyterian minister John Rankin and his wife provided shelter to more than two thousand escaped slaves. The home is currently a museum run by the Ohio Historical Society.

After Abraham Lincoln was elected president in 1860, eleven Southern states seceded from, or left, the Union (another name for the United States at that time). Many white people in these states felt that their way of life was threatened because of Lincoln's opposition to slavery. By the spring of 1861, the Civil War had begun. During the war, about 345,000 Ohioans fought for the North, the most famous of whom was Ulysses S. Grant, who eventually became the commander of all Union armies. Union forces defeated the South in 1865. After the war ended, the Thirteenth Amendment to the U.S. Constitution was adopted, which outlawed slavery throughout the United States.

Political and Industrial Might

After the end of the Civil War, Ohio residents became active leaders in politics and industry. From 1869 to 1881, Ohio sent three of its natives to the White House. U.S. presidents from Ohio who served during this time included Ulysses S. Grant, Rutherford B. Hayes, and James Garfield. In 1870, John D. Rockefeller opened the Standard Oil Company of Ohio, which within a decade owned almost all the country's oil refineries. In 1879, Charles Brush demonstrated his arc streetlights in Cleveland, making it the first city in the country to light its streets using electricity.

Ulysses S. Grant led Union forces during the Civil War. The Ohio native went on to become the eighteenth president of the United States.

Just before the end of the nineteenth century, the Goodyear Tire and Rubber Company opened in Akron. The company was named after Charles Goodyear, who in 1844 developed vulcanization, the process that gives rubber strength. Goodyear manufactured rubber products, such as tires, tubes, and hoses, and it eventually became the nation's largest tire company.

Economic Turmoil

Ohio cities prospered at the beginning of the twentieth century. Tall skyscrapers and other modern office buildings were built. By the 1920s, Cleveland was the fifth-largest city in the United States.

However, in the 1930s, Ohio suffered from the effects of the Great Depression (1929–1939). During this difficult economic period, jobs were scarce and many people suffered greatly. Until then, Ohio had been one of the leading industrial states. It was a tough time for Ohio and the rest of the country. The U.S. government set up programs that hired unemployed workers to build roads, dams, and other projects.

Quick Facts

CLEVELAND'S FOUNDER

Moses Cleaveland of Connecticut founded Cleveland in 1796. According to one legend, the local newspaper at the time dropped the "a" from Cleaveland's name to fit it in a headline.

An increase in manufacturing—and working women—during World War II continued into the 1950s.

World War II

Another major event helped bring economic recovery to Ohio. World War II (1939–1945) was a global conflict and American soldiers and their allies needed food and military equipment. The United States joined the war in 1941 after Japan bombed the U.S. Navy base at Pearl Harbor in Hawaii. Nearly 840,000 Ohioans served in the armed forces. On the home front, women entered the workforce, filling jobs in factories that produced steel, weapons, and aircraft.

After the war, industries continued to grow and more people poured into the state. Cities became so crowded that developers began buying the land around the cities to build homes, and suburbs developed. At this same time, new interstate highways provided quicker routes from one major city to another. By the 1960s, Ohio was one of the most populated states.

A Time of Protests

The 1960s were also a time of turmoil for much of the country. African Americans sought greater equality during the civil rights movement. Sometimes, however, protests turned violent in several major cities, including Cleveland.

At the same time, Americans debated the country's involvement in the Vietnam War. Many Americans opposed the war. In May 1970, perhaps the most famous Vietnam War protest took place at Kent State University near Akron. During the antiwar demonstration, National Guardsmen fatally shot four students and wounded nine others. The tragedy made national headlines and increased support for the antiwar movement.

On May 4, 1970, National Guard troops were called onto the campus of Kent State University to control a crowd of war protesters. The troops fired their weapons into the crowd, killing four protesters.

Workers all over Ohio, including in the state capital of Columbus, are ready to address the challenges of the twenty-first century.

The New Millennium and Beyond

Ohio's large industries improved the economy, but the state's factories also polluted the environment. The plants and animals in Lake Erie were dying from toxic waste being dumped into the water. Then, in 1969, a portion of the Cuyahoga River in Cleveland was so full of chemicals that it actually caught fire. Ohioans realized they had many serious environmental issues to face. Since then, Ohioans have voted to help pay for projects to improve the natural environment. Their efforts have proven successful in many ways. In both Lake Erie and the Cuyahoga River, pollution levels have been substantially reduced.

During the 1980s and 1990s, modern industries began to gain prominence in the state. Computers, automobiles, paper products, and machinery became some of Ohio's top economic drivers.

Today, Ohio finds itself in a time of transition. Once one of the leading industrial giants in the United States, by the early twenty-first century the state had lost many factories as a result of economic failure or relocation to other states and other countries. People dependent on manufacturing jobs for their livelihood often found such jobs to be harder to get. This situation became worse with the onset of difficult economic times that hit the country beginning in late 2007. Like the rest of the United States, Ohio faced one of the toughest economic crises since the Great Depression. With a long and well-preserved history, however, Ohioans know how to face challenges and work to come out ahead.

Important Dates

★ **13,000 BCE–7000 BCE** Paleo-Indians live in present-day Ohio.

★ **8000 BCE–500 BCE** Archaic people hunt and gather in the region's forests.

★ **800 BCE** The Woodland Period, and the mound-building Adena culture, begins.

★ **1000 CE–1600 CE** The Fort Ancient people establish villages in today's Ohio.

★ **1650** The Iroquois begin to claim Ohio land as their hunting grounds.

★ **1669** Frenchman René-Robert Cavelier, sieur de La Salle, explores the Ohio River.

★ **1787** Congress passes the Northwest Ordinance, establishing the Northwest Territory, which includes today's Ohio.

★ **1788** Marietta is established, the first permanent settlement by people of European descent in present-day Ohio.

★ **1794** American Indians lose at the Battle of Fallen Timbers.

★ **1803** Ohio becomes the seventeenth U.S. state.

★ **1816** Columbus is named Ohio's permanent capital.

★ **1832** The Ohio and Erie Canal is completed.

★ **1845** The Miami and Erie Canal opens.

★ **1869** The Cincinnati Red Stockings, later the Cincinnati Reds, become the first professional baseball team.

★ **1962** Astronaut John Glenn, born in Cambridge, becomes the first American to orbit Earth.

★ **1963** The Pro Football Hall of Fame and Museum opens in Canton.

★ **1969** Neil Armstrong, born in Wapakoneta, becomes the first person to walk on the Moon.

★ **1993** Ohio novelist Toni Morrison receives the Nobel Prize for Literature.

★ **1995** The Rock and Roll Hall of Fame and Museum opens in Cleveland.

★ **2010** Ohio teen Anamika Veeramani wins the Scripps National Spelling Bee.

SPIN OUT
SPIN OUT
PLEASE REMOVE
ALL LOOSE ARTICLES
INCLUDING
SANDALS, PHONES,
PAGERS
HATS, PURSES, ETC.
THIS RIDE
TAKES
2 COUPONS
56
54
52
50
48
46
44
40
38
36

The People

Ohio's population has grown over the centuries. In 1800, just three years before Ohio officially became a state, a little more than 45,000 people lived there. As industries boomed in Ohio, so did the population. In 1860, more than 2.4 million people resided in Ohio, making it the third-most-populous state, behind New York and Pennsylvania. By 1900, the population reached 4.2 million people. Fifty years later, close to 8 million people called Ohio home. According to the 2010 Census, Ohio has a little more than 11.5 million residents. Today, the state population is the seventh largest in the country.

So where exactly do all these Ohioans come from? People of many different nationalities and cultures make up the Buckeye State.

American Indians

American Indians were the first people to populate present-day Ohio. Remains of ancient cultures have provided scientists with enough information for them to guess that people lived in this area at least 15,000 years ago. Most of these early people were constantly moving to find food. They survived on their skills as hunters.

By the seventeenth and eighteenth centuries, the largest American Indian groups in what is now Ohio included the Iroquois, Shawnee, Lenape, and Miami.

Thrill rides are among the many attractions at the Ohio State Fair, held each year in Columbus.

Many of these people lived in permanent villages near rivers and streams, for access to fresh water. For food, they hunted and also raised crops. While people were on hunting expeditions, a tent called a tepee gave protection from bad weather.

As white settlers moved into the region, American Indians found their way of life threatened. Although they tried to unite to protect their land and homes, they were unsuccessful. Some American Indians had to move to reservation land in Ohio. By the late 1800s, all reservations in Ohio were closed. Most American Indians were forced to move to reservations in other states.

An American Indian honors his culture at a powwow in Springfield.

Who Ohioans Are

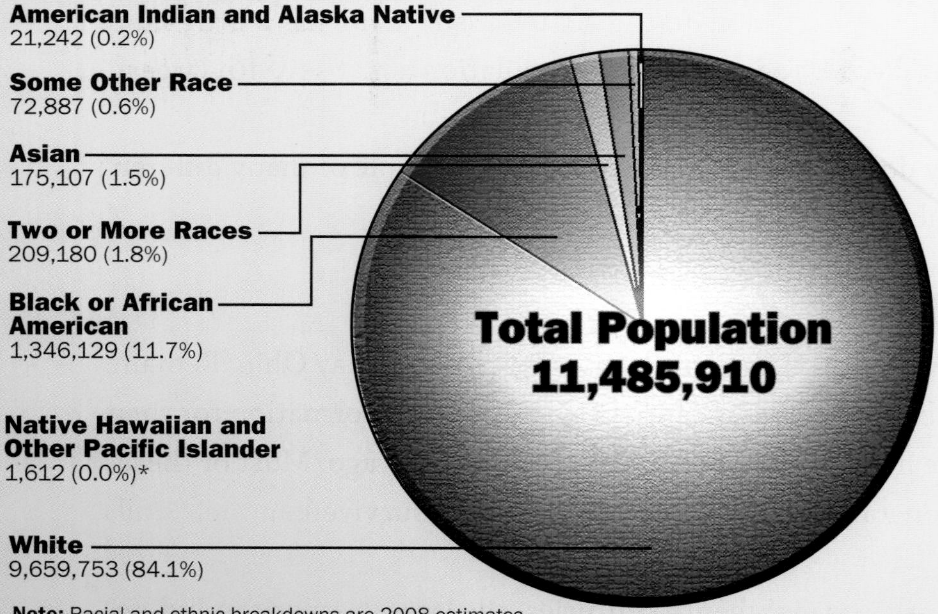

American Indian and Alaska Native
21,242 (0.2%)

Some Other Race
72,887 (0.6%)

Asian
175,107 (1.5%)

Two or More Races
209,180 (1.8%)

Black or African American
1,346,129 (11.7%)

Native Hawaiian and Other Pacific Islander
1,612 (0.0%)*

White
9,659,753 (84.1%)

Total Population
11,485,910

Note: Racial and ethnic breakdowns are 2008 estimates based on Ohio's total estimated population at that time.

Hispanics or Latinos:

- 299,778 people
- 2.6% of the state's population

Hispanics or Latinos may be of any race.

Note: The pie chart shows the racial breakdown of the state's population based on the categories used by the U.S. Bureau of the Census. The Census Bureau reports information for Hispanics or Latinos separately, since they may be of any race. Percentages in the pie chart may not add to 100 because of rounding.

* Less than 0.1%.

Source: U.S. Bureau of the Census, 2008 American Community Survey

The U.S. Census Bureau estimates there are fewer than 22,000 American Indians in Ohio today. They attend school, work, and enjoy the lifestyle that their state offers. Many still practice their traditions. Annual festivals and other gatherings give Ohio's American Indians opportunities to celebrate their history and heritage.

The Europeans

The French were the first Europeans to come to the Ohio area. Most of them were fur trappers, fur traders, or missionaries who came to convert the American Indians to Christianity. After the British won the French and Indian War, they claimed the land that would become Ohio, until the American Revolution. Some former British soldiers settled permanently in the area. After the Revolution, many Americans of English descent began settling in the region.

Many Ohioans trace their roots to European countries. These families in Cleveland enjoy Parade the Circle, a free multicultural celebration held every June.

Today, many Ohioans trace their ancestry back to Europe. Some share the heritage of the early pioneering settlers. Later, people began immigrating to Ohio from throughout Europe.

During the 1840s, people from Ireland came to the United States to escape the Irish potato famine. The failure of the important potato crops caused more than a million people in Ireland to die from starvation and related illnesses. Prejudice against Irish workers, mostly because of their Catholic backgrounds, made it difficult for them to find jobs in the United States. Irish immigrants often had to take tough, poorly paid jobs, such as digging Ohio's canals and laying railroad tracks. Despite these hardships, the Irish immigrants and their work ethic contributed greatly to the growth of the state.

By 1850, almost half of Ohio's immigrant population came from Germany. Most Germans settled around Ohio's major cities. Some were skilled craftspeople who helped create some of Ohio's major buildings. Some cities in Ohio still have large German-American populations. In Cincinnati, for example, almost half of the city's population is descended from German immigrants.

Around 1900, many people in Ohio were of English, German, or Irish descent. But the population was about to become more diverse. By the late 1800s and early 1900s, Russians, Poles, Hungarians, Bulgarians, Croatians, Czechs, Slovaks, and people from other Eastern European areas began settling in Ohio's major cities. Immigrants from Italy and Greece also came in large numbers. So many people were moving to Ohio that, in the early 1900s, almost three-fourths of Cleveland's residents said either they or their parents were born outside the United States.

The Amish Community

The Amish people originally immigrated to the United States from Switzerland during the eighteenth century. Their beliefs differed from other Christian religions in Europe. They came to America seeking religious freedom and a better life. Ohio's Holmes County, located between Columbus and Cleveland, is the home of the largest Amish community in the world. Today, nearly 40,000 Amish people live and work in these rolling hills in eastern Ohio.

Many Amish people do not believe in using modern conveniences such as electricity and automobiles. They dress plainly, practice their traditional ways of life, and live mostly off of the land.

Many Amish believe in a simple lifestyle. A large Amish community lives in eastern Ohio.

Famous Ohioans

Ulysses S. Grant: General and U.S. President

Born in Point Pleasant in 1822, Grant served as the eighteenth president of the United States from 1869 to 1877. During the Civil War, Grant was one of the most successful Union generals, and he rose to become commander of all Union forces. He died in 1885. His body is buried in New York City, in the largest tomb in North America.

Cy Young: Athlete

Denton Young, born in 1867, was an outstanding baseball pitcher for several professional teams, starting with the Cleveland Spiders. The speed and spin on his pitches earned him the nickname "Cy" (for "cyclone"). In his pitching career, he won 511 games, which is still the Major League record. In 1937, he was elected to the Baseball Hall of Fame. The awards given annually to the best pitcher in the American League and in the National League are named the Cy Young Award.

Jesse Owens: Athlete

Born in 1913, Owens was just eight years old when his family moved from Oakville, Alabama, to Cleveland. He attended Fairview Junior High, Cleveland East Technical High School, and Ohio State. Owens became one of the country's greatest track and field stars of all time. In 1936, he won four Olympic gold medals in track and field. In 1976, President Gerald Ford gave Owens the Presidential Medal of Freedom—the nation's highest civilian award.

Neil Armstrong: Astronaut

Born in 1930 in Wapakoneta, Armstrong was a pilot for the U.S. Navy and later a professor of aerospace engineering. As a NASA astronaut, on July 16, 1969, he headed for the Moon aboard the *Apollo 11* spacecraft. Four days later, on July 20, Armstrong became the first person to set foot on the Moon. Named in his honor, the Armstrong Air and Space Museum is located in his hometown.

Maya Lin: Architect

Lin was born in 1959 in Athens. She studied architecture at Yale University. As a student, she entered a national design competition for a memorial for Vietnam War veterans. She was only twenty-one years old when she found out that her design had won. The Vietnam Veterans Memorial in Washington, D.C., was completed in 1982.

Halle Berry: Actress

In 1966, Halle Berry was born in Cleveland. Her parents named her after Halle's, a department store in her hometown. In 2002, she made history as the first African-American woman to win the Academy Award for Best Actress. One of the highest-paid actresses in Hollywood today, she is famous for her role as Storm in the *X-Men* movies.

Born in Lorain, Toni Morrison became the first African American to win the Nobel Prize in Literature.

African Americans

In 1800, only 337 African Americans lived in Ohio, mostly in the southern part of the state. By 1860, a year before the start of the Civil War, more than 36,700 African Americans made Ohio their home. Despite the fact that Ohio was a "free" state, African Americans still faced discrimination. Laws that denied them the right to vote were passed. In parts of southern Ohio, some white people broke the law by owning slaves. To avoid getting caught by authorities, farmers took their slaves to Kentucky to hide them when necessary.

After the Civil War, many African Americans moved to Ohio's cities to find work. Life in the city was not easy for black workers, and well-paid jobs were hard to find.

Today's black Ohioans have prospered and succeeded in various fields. Some notable African Americans from Ohio include Pulitzer Prize winner Rita Dove, who in 1993 became the first

In Their Own Words

Poetry is language at its most distilled and most powerful.

—American poet Rita Dove

African American—and the youngest person—to be named poet laureate of the United States. Also in 1993, Ohioan Toni Morrison became the first African American to receive the Nobel Prize in Literature.

Today, more than 1.3 million African Americans live in the state, making up the largest minority group in Ohio. They represent almost 12 percent of Ohio's population.

Other Cultures

Hispanic Americans and Asian Americans make up the next largest minorities in Ohio. Few Hispanics lived in Ohio until the 1960s. At that time, Latinos began immigrating to the United States in sizable numbers from Central and South American countries, Mexico, and the Caribbean in search of jobs. According to 2008 U.S. Census Bureau estimates, nearly 300,000 Hispanics live in Ohio, accounting for about 2.6 percent of the state's population.

There are more than 175,000 people of Asian descent living in Ohio today, making up about 1.5 percent of the population. They trace their ancestries to China, Japan, India, Korea, the Philippines, Vietnam, and other Asian countries.

Education

Education has always been important to Ohioans. Early settlers built one-room schoolhouses made of logs. Before the first public schools in Ohio were established in 1825, parents paid for their children to attend school, sometimes in the form of goods to the teacher. In 1853, the state's first public high schools opened their doors.

Today, Ohio is home to many well-respected colleges and universities. In 1862, the U.S. Congress passed, and President Lincoln signed, the Morrill Act. This law allowed states to sell large areas

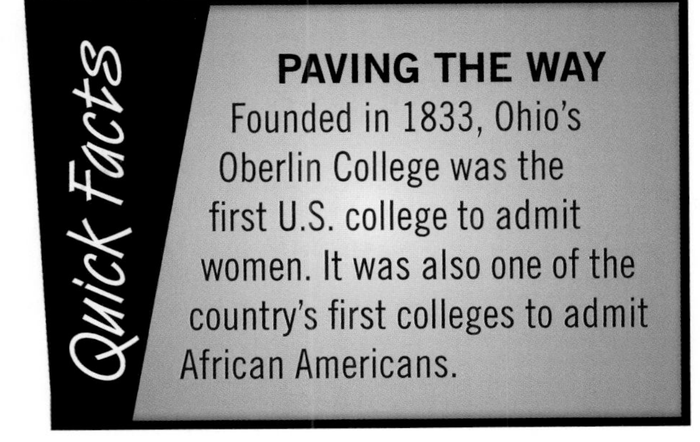

Cleveland State University students celebrate a campus event. Ohio is home to many public and private universities.

of land donated to the states by the federal government in order to raise money to build public colleges. Thanks to this act, the college that is now The Ohio State University, also called Ohio State, was established in Columbus in 1870. Its first class had just twenty-four students. With nearly 60,000 students today, Ohio State has grown into one of the country's largest universities. Other public and private colleges and universities include Ohio University (the state's first public college), Miami University, Oberlin College, Case Western Reserve University, Denison University, and Ohio Wesleyan University.

Students walk across the campus of The Ohio State University in Columbus. It is one of the largest public universities in the country.

Calendar of Events

★ Buzzard Day

Visitors to Hinckley in March can watch as hundreds of turkey vultures, or buzzards, come back to roost in rock cliffs and ledges. These large birds—and their ancestors—have been coming back to Hinckley for at least two hundred years. This annual event marking the beginning of spring is celebrated with bird hikes, songs, stories, crafts, contests, and more.

★ Cleveland International Film Festival

Every March for more than thirty years, Cleveland has hosted a large film festival. People from around the world, including actors and directors, come to watch the premieres of more than 240 movies. The festival has been held at Tower City Cinemas in downtown Cleveland since 1991.

★ Troy Strawberry Festival

Strawberries are an important crop in Ohio, and many towns and cities throughout the state have their own festivals to honor the tasty fruit. But residents of Troy consider their city the Strawberry Capital of Ohio. Each June, Troy's Strawberry Festival draws about 150,000 people.

★ Vectren Dayton Air Show

The Dayton Air Show is considered one of the country's top aviation events. The show, held each July, takes place at Dayton International Airport. The city was the home of brothers Wilbur and Orville Wright, who flew the world's first powered plane in 1903. Visitors can climb aboard some of the historic featured aircraft.

★ All-American Soap Box Derby

Each July, Akron hosts the All-American Soap Box Derby, a racing program in which kids ages nine to sixteen drive homemade cars without engines. It is also known as the Greatest Amateur Racing Event in the World. Winners of local races in the United States and around the world compete in this championship event at the legendary Derby Downs track.

★ The Great Mohican Indian Pow-Wow

In July and September, people gather at the Mohican Reservation Festival Grounds to learn about and celebrate American Indian heritage. This festival in Loudonville includes traditional crafts, dancing, singing, and storytelling.

★ Ohio State Fair

More than 800,000 people attend the annual Ohio State Fair, held in Columbus in early August. For more than 150 years, the fair has celebrated Ohio's products, people, and history. Visitors enjoy live entertainment, thrill rides, prize farm animals, agricultural exhibits, and sculptures made out of butter.

★ Twins Day Festival

Visitors at the Twins Day Festival have to do a double take. Each August, the world's largest gathering of twins and other multiples takes place in Twinsburg. Thirty-seven pairs of twins showed up at the first festival in 1976. Today, about 2,500 sets of multiples attend to enjoy the food, march in the parade, and compete in the talent show.

★ Prairie Peddler Festival

Usually held in late September and early October in Butler, this craft festival gives visitors a feel of Ohio life from pioneer days. At this family-friendly gathering, visitors can enjoy entertainment, food, and displays of handmade crafts.

How the Government Works

Ohio's constitution was first created in 1802, one year before Ohio was admitted to the Union. The constitution affirms that the state government should be divided into three separate branches. The executive branch administers state laws, the legislative branch makes laws, and the judicial branch enforces and interprets laws. The state government is centered in the state capital, Columbus.

Each of Ohio's eighty-eight counties, as well as each town and city, has a local government. An elected board of commissioners governs most counties. Many of Ohio's cities elect a mayor who enforces local laws passed by a council and manages the city government's budget.

Various taxes help fund state and local governments. Residents often have to pay property, income, and sales taxes. Property taxes are based on the value of a person's home or other personal possessions, such as an automobile. When people buy certain products at a store, they pay a sales tax that might go partly to the state government and partly to the local government. State and other income taxes are taken out of a worker's paycheck or paid directly by people who are self-employed. State and local taxes help pay for schools, police and fire departments, town and state buildings, public libraries, and all kinds of government services, such as snow removal in the winter and lifeguards at public pools in the summer.

Lawmakers meet inside the Ohio Statehouse in Columbus.

A statue of Christopher Columbus stands in front of City Hall in Columbus. The capital city was named after the famous explorer.

Quick Facts

MOTHER OF U.S. PRESIDENTS

Ohio is often called the Mother of U.S. Presidents. Seven presidents were born in Ohio: Ulysses S. Grant (18th), Rutherford B. Hayes (19th), James Garfield (20th), Benjamin Harrison (23rd), William McKinley (25th), William Howard Taft (27th), and Warren G. Harding (29th). William Henry Harrison (9th) was born in Virginia but lived in Ohio when he ran for president.

Branches of Government

EXECUTIVE ★ ★ ★ ★ ★ ★ ★ ★

The governor is the head of the executive branch. The governor is responsible for managing a legislature-approved state budget, signing bills that are passed in the legislature, and appointing the directors of state departments and agencies. The governor is elected to a four-year term. He or she can serve only two terms in a row.

LEGISLATIVE ★ ★ ★ ★ ★ ★ ★ ★

Ohio's legislature is called the general assembly. It has two houses, or chambers: the house of representatives and the senate. When the first meeting of the general assembly was held in Chillicothe on March 1, 1803, there were only thirty representatives in the house and fourteen members in the senate. In 1967, voters approved an amendment to the state constitution to increase those numbers. Now, Ohio has ninety-nine members in the house and thirty-three members in the senate. State senators may serve no more than two four-year terms. State representatives may serve no more than four two-year terms. The main role of these legislators is to debate and vote on proposed laws (bills). If the general assembly votes in favor of a bill, the governor may sign it into law.

JUDICIAL ★ ★ ★ ★ ★ ★ ★ ★ ★

This branch is made up of the Ohio supreme court and many lower courts, including courts of appeals, courts of common pleas, county courts, municipal courts, and the court of claims. The main job of the state supreme court judges is to rule on cases in which a lower court's decision has been appealed by the losing party. State supreme court judges can decide whether or not a state law agrees with the state constitution. They also review all death penalty cases. One chief justice and six justices sit on the supreme court. They can be elected to an unlimited number of six-year terms.

Representation in Washington, D.C.

Like all Americans, the people of Ohio are represented in the U.S. Congress in Washington, D.C. Each state elects two U.S. senators, who serve six-year terms. There is no limit on the number of terms a U.S. senator can serve. A state's population determines the number of people that it sends to the U.S. House of Representatives. After the 2010 Census, Ohio was entitled to sixteen representatives in the House. They can be elected to an unlimited number of two-year terms.

Quick Facts

SPACE SENATOR

John H. Glenn Jr. was born on July 18, 1921, in Cambridge, Ohio. In 1962, he became the first American astronaut to orbit Earth. After retiring as an astronaut, he represented Ohio as a U.S. senator from 1974 to 1999. In 1998, at age seventy-seven, he returned to space, becoming the oldest person to travel outside Earth's atmosphere.

How a Bill Becomes a Law

Members of the house and senate may either create new laws or change old ones. A law begins as a bill proposed by a state representative or a state senator. But the idea for a bill may come from an Ohio citizen. Any state resident with an idea for a new law can present it to his or her legislator.

In the legislature, a representative's or senator's proposal is written in legal language, recorded, and then considered. A bill introduced by a representative is first considered in the house, and a bill introduced by a senator is first considered in the senate.

First, the bill is debated by a committee of legislators. The committee might hold hearings to find out what members of the public and groups interested in the subject of the bill think about it. If the committee approves the bill, it is next debated in the full house or senate. If the members of that chamber pass the bill by a majority vote, it goes to the other chamber, where the process of considering and voting on the bill is repeated.

If the second chamber passes the bill but makes changes to it first, then usually a committee made up of three members from each chamber works to come up with a final version of the bill. This final version must be passed again by both the house and the senate.

Contacting Lawmakers

★ ★ ★ ★ ★ ★ ★ ★ ★ ★ ★ ★

Ohioans can take an active role in government and contact their representative and senator about issues of concern. Legislators are there to serve Ohioans and the state. To contact Ohio state legislators, go to

http://www.legislature.state.oh.us

Enter your zip code or district number to find your senator or representative.

Once both chambers have approved a bill in exactly the same form, it is sent to the governor for his or her signature. If the governor signs the bill (or takes no action on it for ten days), it becomes a law. However, the governor may also veto, or reject, the bill if he or she does not agree with it. In that case, either the bill dies, or it may still become a law if both houses of the legislature again vote in favor of it—but this time by at least a three-fifths majority.

Visitors tour the inside of the Ohio Statehouse.

Making a Living

The two main industries in Ohio's economic history are agriculture and manufacturing. Since the first permanent settlers in the Ohio region planted and cultivated seeds, agriculture has helped Ohioans make a living. Today, Ohio's farm products are used throughout the state, as well as exported to other states and countries.

Agriculture

Agriculture in Ohio has gone through good and bad times since statehood. The Great Depression hit Ohio farmers at the same time as a very long drought that caused crops to die. World War II, on the other hand, increased the demand for food, which benefited Ohio farmers. In the second half of the twentieth century, however, the number of farms in Ohio declined. The cost of food fell while the cost of living rose. Farmers were getting less for their crops at the same time that they were paying more for clothing, electricity, and machinery. In time, many people sold their farms and moved to the cities.

Quick Facts

FARM FESTIVAL

One of Ohio's popular agricultural celebrations is the annual Bob Evans Farm Festival in Rio Grande. In 1948, Bob Evans (1918–2007) started making sausage from hogs raised on his farm. He opened the first Bob Evans Restaurant in 1962 in Rio Grande. Today, the chain has restaurants in more than twenty states.

Agriculture plays a key role in Ohio's economy.

Workers & Industries

Industry	Number of People Working in That Industry	Percentage of All Workers Who Are Working in That Industry
Education and health care	1,276,511	23.0%
Manufacturing	910,430	16.4%
Wholesale and retail businesses	806,779	14.5%
Publishing, media, entertainment, hotels, and restaurants	587,326	10.6%
Professionals, scientists, and managers	503,972	9.1%
Banking and finance, insurance, and real estate	359,367	6.4%
Construction	318,770	5.7%
Transportation and public utilities	288,997	5.2%
Other services	244,893	4.4%
Government	206,160	3.7%
Farming, forestry, fishing, and mining	56,459	1.0%
Totals	**5,559,664**	**100%**

Notes: Figures above do not include people in the armed forces. "Professionals" includes people such as doctors and lawyers. Percentages may not add to 100 because of rounding.

Source: U.S. Bureau of the Census, 2008 estimates

Dairy cattle, found on many Ohio farms, graze in a field of wildflowers.

Ohio still has about 80,000 farms, which cover about half the state. The major crops include soybeans, corn, hay, oats, and wheat. Most of these grains are fed to cattle, another important agricultural product. Ohio's cattle provide milk and beef. Ohio also is a major producer of hogs, ranks very high in the production of eggs, and makes more Swiss cheese than any other state.

RECIPE FOR SPICY APPLE CIDER

During the early 1800s, Ohio's own Johnny Appleseed planted apple trees throughout the landscape. On a cold evening, nothing tastes better than a cup of hot spicy apple cider. Ask an adult to help you to prepare this easy, delicious drink.

WHAT YOU NEED

1 gallon (3.8 liters) apple cider or apple juice

10 whole cloves

3 cinnamon sticks

1 tablespoon (12 grams) sugar

1 fresh lemon

Pour the apple cider into a large pot on the stove. Add the whole cloves and the cinnamon sticks. Sprinkle the sugar into the pot and stir. Ask an adult to help you cut the fresh lemon and squeeze its juice into the pot.

Put the burner on a low heat and let the apple cider cook. Stir the mixture every 15 minutes to make sure that the liquid is not sticking to the bottom of the pot. After 1 hour, turn off the burner and let the cider cool down for a few minutes.

Ask an adult to pour the cider through a strainer into a large container. The strainer will catch the lemon seeds, cloves, and pieces of cinnamon sticks. After you enjoy your hot cup of spicy apple cider, store the rest of the cider in the refrigerator. When you want another cup, you can heat it up again on the stove or in a microwave.

Apples are another important state product. Ohioans are very proud of their famous apple farmer, John Chapman (1774–1845), known as Johnny Appleseed. Legend says that when Ohio first became a state, Johnny Appleseed was traveling all over the region, planting apple orchards. Some of those trees, now two hundred years old, continue to bear fruit. The Johnny Appleseed Educational Center and Museum on the campus of Urbana University in Urbana honors the legendary frontiersman. Outside the museum are apple trees that started as cuttings from trees planted by Johnny Appleseed.

Ohio farmers also produce grapes and strawberries. Vegetables such as cucumbers and tomatoes are major crops in Ohio as well.

In the early 1800s, John Chapman, known as Johnny Appleseed, traveled around the American frontier planting apple seeds.

Manufacturing

Like agriculture, manufacturing has played a major role in the state economy. Ohio is a leading manufacturer of cars, trucks, motor vehicle parts, jet engines, airplane parts, and other transportation equipment. Some Ohioans work in factories that produce steel and tools. Ohio is one of the top steel-producing states in the country.

Ohio has many different kinds of factories. The city of Napoleon, for example, is home to the world's largest soup factory. Wellston claims to be the world's leading producer of frozen pizzas. Cincinnati has the biggest soap factory in the United States. Other major products made in Ohio include computer parts, rubber, electrical equipment, clay, glass, and paper and plastic items.

Many food-processing plants in Ohio handle the products that are grown on Ohio's farms. Some types of food-processing plants include those that pack meat, preserve and can fruits, and make dairy products.

Automobile manufacturing is among Ohio's leading industries.

Mining

Mining also contributes to the state's economy. Ohio is one of the country's top coal-mining states. Coal is the state's most valuable mineral. Oil, natural gas, salt, clay, sandstone, and other minerals are also mined in Ohio. Sandstone and other minerals are used to construct buildings and highways.

A bulldozer moves coal at a mine in Powhatan.

Products & Resources

Soybeans

Soybeans are Ohio's top crop. Although most of the state's soybeans are fed to cattle, some are used to make a nondairy substitute for milk. In addition, soybeans are used in nonfood items such as hand cleaners, chemical cleaners, and lubricants that help machines run smoothly.

Corn

Corn—one of Ohio's largest crops—is grown throughout the state. It is Ohio's second most-valuable crop, after soybeans. Ohio ranks among the top ten corn-producing states in the country. Most of this corn is not eaten by people, though. More than half goes to feeding livestock, such as cows. Corn is also used to make a variety of products from plastic and ethanol (a type of fuel) to cereal and cooking oil to glue and ink.

Strawberries

Ohio farmers rank tenth in the United States for growing strawberries. More than 710 acres (287 hectares) of farmland are devoted just to strawberries. About 3 million pounds (1.4 million kilograms) of strawberries were produced in 2009. Strawberries are sometimes hard to grow. But Ohio's university researchers are working to find new types of strawberries to boost the state's production of this tasty fruit.

Coal

Coal is Ohio's most important mined resource. Most coal is mined in the eastern part of the state. Although miners have been digging for coal for a long time, scientists believe more than 20 billion tons (18 billion metric tons) of coal remain buried underground.

Salt

When heavy snow falls on Ohio's roads, trucks hurry out to spread salt on the pavement and melt the snow away. Where does all that salt come from? Northeast Ohio is home to large deposits of salt about 2,000 feet (600 m) underground. Ohio is one of the country's largest producers of rock salt. The state mines about 4 million tons (3.6 million t) each year.

Motor Vehicles

Automobile manufacturing is a $19.3 billion annual industry in the state. That is about 13 percent of total U.S. output. Ohio is the second-largest producer of motor vehicles in the United States, after Michigan. Ranking behind Michigan and Indiana, Ohio employs the most workers in automobile manufacturing.

The Business of Service

Most workers in Ohio have jobs in the service industry. This industry includes banking, health care, education, restaurants, retail stores, and hotels.

Tourism is a major part of the state's service industry as well. Each year, millions of people visit Ohio. Tourists relax on Ohio's lakeshore, hike through its parks, or visit the state's many historic sites and museums. Others enjoy the different festivals, fairs, and other events in Ohio's cities and towns. All these people spend money in the state. That money provides a profit for many service businesses and, when tourists make purchases, sales tax revenue for the state government and local governments. The tourism industry also employs many Ohioans, including tour guides, museum curators, hotel clerks, waitstaff, and store clerks.

Tourist Attractions

Tourists visiting Ohio have plenty to keep them busy. The state is home to many exciting historical, cultural, and recreational attractions. Tourists flock to Cedar Point Amusement Park in Sandusky in northern Ohio. Officially called "The Roller Coaster Capital of the World," Cedar Point holds the world record for the most roller coasters in one park—seventeen in all. Home to seventy-five rides as of 2010, Cedar Point now boasts more rides than any other amusement park in the world.

Quick Facts

ROCK AND ROLL ROOTS

In the 1950s, Cleveland disc jockey Alan Freed coined the phrase "rock and roll." Ohio is also the only state that has an official rock song. "Hang on Sloopy" was written in the 1960s by a Dayton band called the McCoys. The Ohio State University Marching Band plays the song at Buckeye football games.

Zoos are another state attraction. The Cincinnati Zoo and Botanical Garden is the second-oldest zoo in the United States. Animal lovers can also visit zoos in Columbus, Toledo, and Cleveland.

Cedar Point in Sandusky has more roller coasters than any other amusement park in the world. The park, opened in 1870, is one of North America's oldest.

Ohio is home to several "halls of fame." The Rock and Roll Hall of Fame and Museum, located on Lake Erie in downtown Cleveland, opened in 1995. The museum's attention-grabbing glass pyramid attracts more than 7.5 million people each year. Visitors learn about the histories of their favorite rock stars and get an up-close look at music memorabilia. Sports fans and motorcycle enthusiasts can head to Canton's Pro Football Hall of Fame or the Motorcycle Hall of Fame Museum in Pickerington.

Historic Ohio draws tourists of all ages. The state pays homage to some of its flight pioneers with the Armstrong Air and Space Museum in Wapakoneta and the National Museum of the U.S. Air Force in Dayton. The Air Force museum includes exhibits on the Wright brothers.

Other famous Ohio natives have museums dedicated in their honor. Tourists can visit the Thomas Edison Birthplace Museum in Milan and learn about the inventor of the light bulb, the record player, and the motion-picture camera. The life of one of history's greatest golfers is chronicled at the Jack Nicklaus Museum in his hometown of Columbus.

Science buffs can get their fill at the Goodyear World of Rubber in Akron or the Toledo Center of Science and Industry. Nature lovers can enjoy underground caves at Seneca Caverns in Bellevue or waterfalls and hiking at Wayne National Forest or Hocking Hills State Park in southeastern Ohio.

Professional sports provide enjoyment for Ohio residents and visitors alike. Ohio has teams in all four major professional sports. Columbus has hockey's Blue Jackets. Cincinnati is home to baseball's Reds and football's Bengals. Cleveland

In Their Own Words

As a boy, because I was born and raised in Ohio, about 60 miles [97 km] north of Dayton, the legends of the Wrights have been in my memories as long as I can remember.

—Neil Armstrong, first person to walk on the Moon

Kids enjoy one of many colorful exhibits at the Rock and Roll Hall of Fame and Museum in downtown Cleveland.

A high school softball team celebrates in front of a statue of Hall of Fame pitcher Bob Feller at Progressive Field, home of the Cleveland Indians.

has baseball's Indians, basketball's Cavaliers, and football's Browns.

The Ohio State University competes in more than two dozen varsity sports and has one of the top-ranked football teams in the country. The Buckeyes play in the state's largest stadium.

The Future

Like residents of many other states, Ohioans are trying to protect their environment and, at the same time, encourage growth. More businesses might mean more jobs and money, but do they also mean more pollution and damage to the natural environment? Developing high-technology and other "clean" industries may help Ohioans to have comfortable lives and still preserve the beauty of their state.

State Flag & Seal

Ohio's flag is shaped like a pennant with red and white stripes and a large blue triangle. The triangle has seventeen white stars in it. The thirteen stars grouped around the circle represent the thirteen original colonies. The other four white stars near the corner of the triangle symbolize Ohio becoming the seventeenth state. The white "O" stands for "Ohio," and the red center symbolizes the buckeye. The blue triangle represents the state's hills and valleys. The red and white stripes stand for Ohio's roads and waterways.

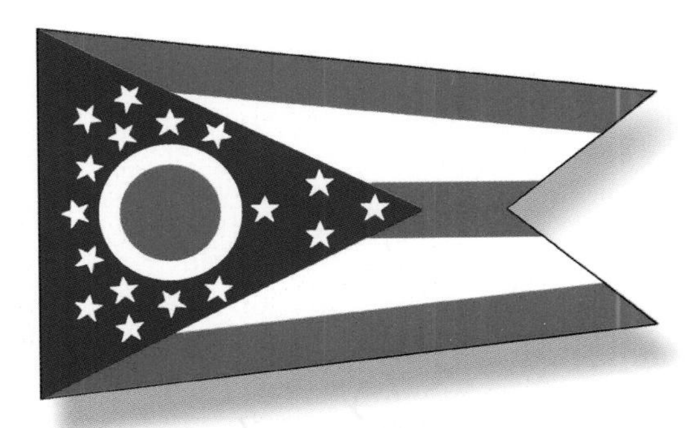

The Ohio state seal depicts a rising sun with thirteen rays, representing the original colonies. The sun is rising over Mount Logan. In the middle ground is the Scioto River. There is also a bundle of wheat, which stands for Ohio's agriculture and bounty. Next to the wheat is a bundle of seventeen arrows, which refer to Ohio's being the seventeenth state to join the Union.

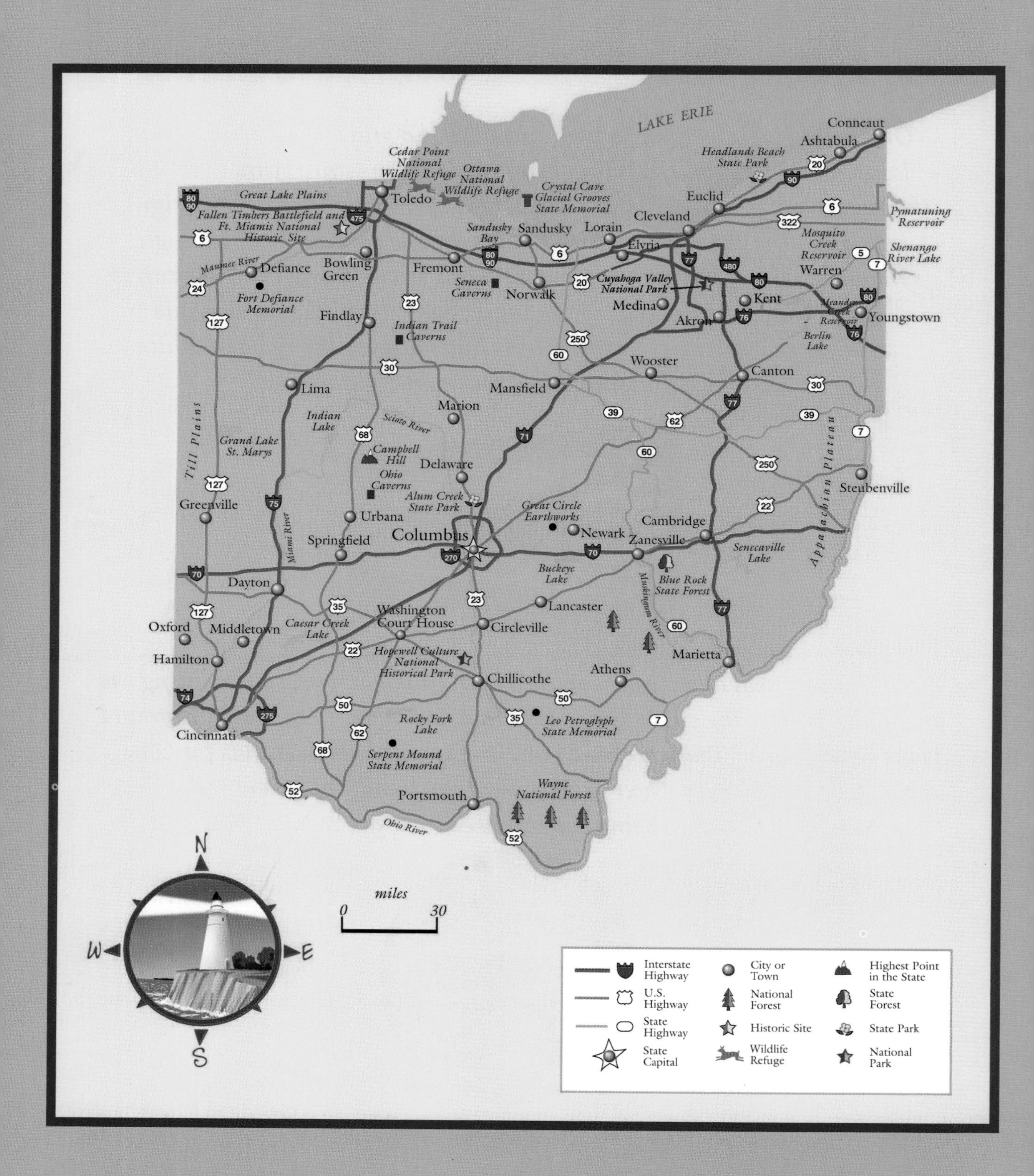
LAKE ERIE
Conneaut
Ashtabula
Headlands Beach State Park
Euclid
Cleveland
Lorain
Elyria
Sandusky
Sandusky Bay
Cedar Point National Wildlife Refuge
Ottawa National Wildlife Refuge
Crystal Cave Glacial Grooves State Memorial
Toledo
Great Lake Plains
Fallen Timbers Battlefield and Ft. Miamis National Historic Site
Maumee River
Defiance
Fort Defiance Memorial
Bowling Green
Fremont
Seneca Caverns
Norwalk
Cuyahoga Valley National Park
Medina
Akron
Kent
Warren
Youngstown
Pymatuning Reservoir
Mosquito Creek Reservoir
Shenango River Lake
Berlin Lake
Findlay
Indian Trail Caverns
Wooster
Canton
Mansfield
Lima
Marion
Indian Lake
Sciota River
Till Plains
Grand Lake St. Marys
Campbell Hill
Ohio Caverns
Delaware
Alum Creek State Park
Greenville
Urbana
Springfield
Columbus
Great Circle Earthworks
Newark
Cambridge
Zanesville
Steubenville
Appalachian Plateau
Senecaville Lake
Miami River
Dayton
Buckeye Lake
Blue Rock State Forest
Muskingum River
Lancaster
Washington Court House
Circleville
Oxford
Middletown
Caesar Creek Lake
Hamilton
Hopewell Culture National Historical Park
Chillicothe
Athens
Marietta
Cincinnati
Rocky Fork Lake
Leo Petroglyph State Memorial
Serpent Mound State Memorial
Portsmouth
Wayne National Forest
Ohio River
N
S
E
W
miles
0
30
Interstate Highway
U.S. Highway
State Highway
State Capital
City or Town
National Forest
Historic Site
Wildlife Refuge
Highest Point in the State
State Forest
State Park
National Park

State Song

Beautiful Ohio

words by Ballard MacDonald
music by Robert King

BOOKS

Barker, Charles Ferguson. *Under Ohio: The Story of Ohio's Rocks and Fossils*. Athens, OH: Ohio University Press, 2007.

Hudson, Wade. *The Underground Railroad*. Danbury, CT: Children's Press, 2007.

Koestler-Grack, Rachel A. *Neil Armstrong*. Pleasantville, NY: Gareth Stevens, 2010.

McHugh, Erin. *State Shapes: Ohio*. New York: Black Dog & Leventhal Publishers, 2007.

Stewart, Mark. *The Ohio State Buckeyes*. Chicago: Norwood House, 2009.

WEBSITES

Discover Ohio:
http://consumer.discoverohio.com

Ohio Department of Natural Resources:
http://www.ohiodnr.gov

Ohio.gov—the Official State Website:
http://ohio.gov

Ohio History Central:
http://www.ohiohistorycentral.org

Ohio Kids:
http://www.ohiokids.org

Ohio Memory—Documenting the State's History:
http://www.ohiomemory.org

Joyce Hart fell in love with writing while she was a student at the University of Oregon. She raised her children in Eugene and is currently a freelance writer and the author of six books. For the past twenty years she has enjoyed traveling the back roads of the Pacific Northwest.

Lisa M. Herrington is a children's writer and editor. She has made several trips to Ohio to visit her husband's family, natives of the Cleveland and Youngstown areas. She has enjoyed spending time along Lake Erie, visiting the Rock and Roll Hall of Fame and Museum, soaking up the unique Cleveland architecture, and admiring the murals at the Lakewood Public Library. She lives in Trumbull, Connecticut, with her husband, Ryan, and daughter, Caroline.
She dedicates this book to her extended Ohio family.

INDEX

Page numbers in **boldface** are illustrations.

INDEX